Our Little Saxon Cousin of Long Ago

This edition published 2026
by Living Book Press
Copyright © Living Book Press, 2026

ISBN: 978-1-76183-155-3 (hardcover)
        978-1-76183-152-2 (softcover)

First published in 1916.

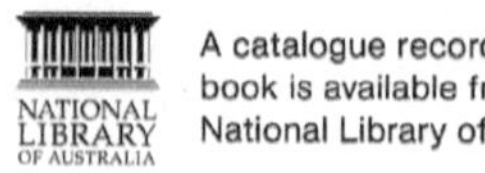

A catalogue record for this book is available from the National Library of Australia

Our Little Saxon Cousin of Long Ago

by

Julia Darrow Cowles

"TURGAR LAID HIS HAND WITH A GESTURE
OF AFFECTION UPON HIS BRACELET."

Contents

CHAPTER I
Turgar's Home

It was a rude sort of home, yet strongly built. The stones which formed its walls had been torn away from the ruined turrets of an old Roman watch tower. The thralls of Wulstan had laid them.

The walls of the house were solid and heavy. All the light that made its way into the rooms came through narrow spaces left for the purpose between some of the stones. But rude though it was, it was a home of unusual comfort and refinement for the time. The ends of the wooden benches about the fireplace were carved with the figures and heads of animals; skins were thrown across the benches and upon the floor; and pieces of fine embroidery covered the cushions.

The home was in Saxon England, in the year 868, when Ethelred was King, and the young Prince Alfred had yet to earn his title of Alfred the Great.

Upon one of the skins spread upon the floor a boy lay stretched at full length, his chin propped in his hands, and his eyes gazing dreamily into the glowing fire. It was plainly to be seen that his thoughts were far away.

Presently he brought himself to a sitting posture, and, swaying his strong lithe body in time to the cadence of the music, he began to sing:

> Once on a time it happened that we,
>   on our vessel,
> Ventured to ride o'er the billows,
>   the high dashing surges.

As the notes of the stirring song rang out, the great dog, which had been lying beside him, stirred, stretched himself, then sat upon his haunches as though ready to bound forth at a word.

The boy gave a sympathetic nod to the dog and continued his song:

> Full of danger to us were the paths of the ocean—

But just as he finished the third line a gust of wind came through the hole in the roof above the fireplace, carrying with it a swirling cloud of smoke, which, for the moment, filled the room and threatened to choke both boy and dog.

"Ugh, what a way for the wind to treat us," spluttered the boy. "It must be a wild night outside."

As he spoke, a hand drew aside the heavy tapestry

in the doorway, and a stately, graceful woman entered the room. She was tall, and her gown of rich blue was embroidered with threads of gold, while a wide mantle was drawn about her waist and over her left shoulder, its ends falling almost to the hem of her dress. Upon her shoulder a jeweled clasp held the mantle in place.

"Mother," said the boy, jumping to his feet as she entered, "sit on this side of the fire-place, where the smoke is not so bad. It is a wild night, and father will have a hard ride to the castle."

"You are right, Turgar," replied Gyneth. "I wish he might have put off going till the morning; but it was the King's business, and that brooks no delay."

"The Danes are not fighting, are they?" questioned Turgar anxiously.

"No," answered his mother, "the Danes are quiet and in their camps; but the young Prince Alfred is soon to wed, and King Ethelred has matters to bring before his thanes."

"And are you not going to the wedding of the Prince?" asked Turgar.

"Yes," was the reply, "your father and I are asked, and so is your brother Withgar, but the wedding will not take place for a number of days. Your father will return for me."

Turgar Jumped To His Feet With Clenched Fists.

"Oh, I wish I could see the wedding of the Prince!" exclaimed Turgar, with sparkling eyes. And then he added more quietly, and. with a slight flush, "He is my hero, mother! Did you know that he was my hero?"

"He may well be," answered Gyneth, laying her hand lovingly upon Turgar's head. "Your father thinks him a wonderful youth. He is both honorable in his dealings and wise in counsel. I am glad he is your hero."

Turgar dropped upon his knee before his mother and was about to ask for a story of his hero, when there was a sudden commotion outside.

The dogs in the yard began barking; the servants cried, "Hi, hi, who comes?"

Gyneth's face grew pale. Turgar jumped to his feet with clenched fists, and the great dog beside him, though he made no sound, drew back his lips in an ugly snarl, while the hair along his spine stood erect with bristling fierceness.

"The Danes!" This was the thought which shot through every mind—even the dogs seemed to know the word—for a band of these pirates and free-booters from the north was encamped in the country to the south, near the coast, where they proposed to spend the winter. They had promised to leave the Saxons in peace, but the promise of a Dane was easily broken, and the people were in constant dread of a sudden raid.

But as the little group in the home of Wulstan stood with suspended breath, waiting to know the cause of the sudden outcry, they heard a shout of welcome, a friendly calling and answering, and their tense attitudes relaxed. It proved to be a belated band of hunters returning from the chase. Among them was Withgar, Turgar's older brother. He had killed a wild boar in the forest and was dragging it home.

Turgar dashed out to meet him, and a few moments later the two brothers entered the room where Gyneth sat.

"Oh, Withgar, do tell us of the hunt," cried Turgar. "I shall be so glad when I am old enough to go with you!"

Withgar smiled at the boy's eagerness as he said, "We had rare sport, though for a time I was not sure whether I was to get the boar, or the boar was to get me.

"I came upon it suddenly, and the horse that I was riding was not used to the hunt. Then my spear broke when I thrust at the boar and he turned and charged me. But luckily Acca was near, and a better thrall it would be hard to find. I shouted for his spear, when mine broke, and, balancing it well, he threw it to me and I caught it, though my horse was plunging badly. In a trice I gave the boar another thrust and made an end of him. And now," he added lightly, "we shall have plenty of meat, and you will be glad of that, Turgar, I know."

Turgar's eyes shone like twin stars when Withgar finished, and it was clear that he was not thinking then of the boar's meat.

"Good! Good!" he cried.

To himself he said, "Oh, I do hope that I, too, may have great adventures, when I grow up.

And Turgar's wish was to be fulfilled in generous measure.

CHAPTER II

THE STORY OF A WONDERFUL JOURNEY

The Saxons were a restless people, and the men of the leading families seldom stayed long at home. The craftsmen, and those who tilled the fields, worked steadily enough, but the men of large estates, who had received their lands in return for services rendered the King, were constantly moving about.

Wulstan was a thane, a counselor of the King, and Withgar was a soldier, so Turgar and his mother were often left alone with the servants.

There was plenty going on about the place to entertain a young boy, and Turgar often occupied himself by going from one group of workmen to another. He watched the smith as he fashioned the implements for tilling the soil, or made knives for the use of Withgar in his hunting, or spear heads and swords for the soldiers.

At other times he watched the women gathering honey from the hives, for honey was the only sweetening of those days, and the keeping of bees was an important part of the farm industries.

Turgar was always eager to do something, and sometimes the smith would let him try his hand at beating the metal, or polishing the implements that had not too sharp an edge. Then they would talk together about Prince Alfred, or the Danes, or the old tales of early history and legend.

These old stories had a fascination for Turgar, and he often wished that he had some one to talk with who knew more about the true history of the country than the smith knew. When he asked, "Who built the old stone towers, such as our house is made from?" or "Why cannot we Saxons make splendid roads like the bit of road that lies to the west of us?" the smith would answer, "They say that the Romans built the towers and the roads, and they must have been master workmen, but who they were or where they came from I do not know."

When Wulstan was at home Turgar asked him many questions about the Romans, and Wulstan could tell wonderful stories; but he was not at home long at a time, and when he was at home there were many matters about the farm to keep him busy.

Turgar's mother, Gyneth, was a woman much above the average of her time, but she did not read or write, and neither in fact did Wulstan. Indeed, there were very few people in the land who could. Gyneth had a good memory and she had learned much about the history of the country through the stories which had been handed down from one generation to another, and through the songs and tales of the minstrels who wandered about from castle to camp, and from camp to castle. These minstrels were welcomed wherever they went, and earned their living by means of their stories and songs.

History, preserved only by such means as these, could not be very accurate, and its heroes were sure to be given more than mortal honors as one after another told the tale of their brave deeds; but all early history has been handed down in this same fashion.

Gyneth could not tell Turgar much about the Romans, but she knew the stories of her own time and her own people, as well as the legends of the gods of Asgard.

One day Turgar came to her, carrying in his hand a trinket which the goldsmith had just made for him. "May I have a chain, mother," he asked, "so that I may wear the charm about my neck? The goldsmith told me that Prince Alfred always wears a charm, and that his mother gave it to him when he was a very little boy."

Gyneth laid aside her embroidery while she selected a light chain which she fastened about Turgar's neck, with the new ornament attached to it. Then she said, "Yes, Turgar, I have heard about Prince Alfred's charm. His mother had it made for him, and she placed it about his neck just before he left her to go on his long pilgrimage to Rome.”

“Oh, do tell me all about it!” cried Turgar. “How old was the Prince then?”

“He was five years old,” answered Gyneth; “a very little boy to go on so long and perilous a pilgrimage. But he was put in the care of the good bishop Swithin, who watched over him like a father.”

“And is it a long way to Rome?” asked Turgar, for, since there were no schools in the land of the Anglo-Saxons, Turgar had not the remotest idea of geography.

“Yes, it is a long way,” replied Gyneth. “The little Prince had to travel first on horseback to the sea, then in vessels with big brightly colored sails, and, after that, on horseback again. Part of the way they passed over mountains where the paths were steep and narrow, and where bands of robbers were hiding. But King Ethelwolf, his father, knew of these perils, and so he sent a whole troop of thanes and priests, of soldiers and horsemen and thralls to guard the Prince, for he knew that no band of robbers would dare to assail so large a number of men.”

“How long were they on the way?” asked Turgar.

“Many, many weeks,” replied his mother. “They took great stores of food and goods with them, and always they looked out for the little Prince first. They had furs to wrap him in when the weather was cold, and the bishop and his nurse were always close beside him to see that he did not grow too tired, or lack for any good thing that they could furnish. But even then the pilgrimage was long and tiresome.

"Here and there on the way they came to great walled castles, and then they stopped for several days to rest, for the owners of the castles were glad to have a royal guest, even though he were but a little boy.

"At last they reached Rome, where they could rest for a long time. They had brought rich gifts to the Pope, Leo IV, and he was especially pleased with the little Prince who had come so far to see him."

"What did they take to the Pope?" questioned Turgar.

"There were vessels of gold and of silver set with precious jewels. There were robes of great beauty, embroidered in gold and precious stones, and there were gifts of money for schools and churches."

"I am so glad the Pope liked the Prince, said Turgar; then he added hastily, "but he could not help it."

Gyneth smiled. "He liked him so well," she said, "that he anointed him, it is said, with holy oil, and told him that he would one day be King."

"Oh," cried Turgar, "did he say that? And Alfred is

not the eldest son. Oh, I am glad! I wish I could help to make it come true."

"Perhaps you can," said Gyneth, "if it proves to be for the good of the country. Every man can help his country and his King by being brave and true. There is no telling what your chance may be when you are grown. But you can be ready for it by being strong and courageous and faithful each day."

"Must I wait till I am grown?" asked Turgar.

"What could a boy do?" asked his mother. "I do not know," said Turgar, "but sometimes boys can help if they are brave."

CHAPTER III

"My Prince"

The wedding of Prince Alfred to Elswitha had been heralded throughout the land. Wulstan, Gyneth, and their elder son, Withgar, had, as we know, been bidden to the castle of King Ethelred to witness the event, and to take part in the festival which would follow.

"Oh, I do wish I were as old as Withgar!" exclaimed Turgar vehemently, bringing his foot down upon the stone flagging of the floor as he spoke. He thought himself alone, but a hearty, laughing voice responded, "And why are you so eager to be of Withgar's age?"

"Oh, Father!" exclaimed Turgar, recognizing the voice, although he had not known of his father's return, "I want to witness the wedding of my Prince. I want to look upon him just once. I am sure if I could only see him it would help me to be true and brave always."

"Why!" exclaimed his father, "I did not know you were so fond of Prince Alfred. How do you happen to know so much about him?"

"Oh," said Turgar, "long ago I heard Withgar telling

of a hunt in which he and the Prince took part. It ended in a battle with a party of Danes, and oh! the Prince was wonderful. Withgar said they came upon the Danes just as they were about to set fire to a farmhouse, and a woman and a young girl were shut inside the house. The Prince fought like a young lion, and he alone killed three of the Danes, and he set the woman and girl free. The others of the hunting party settled the rest of the Danes and put out the fire. Oh, it was glorious, the way Withgar told it, and the Prince has been my hero ever since!"

"That was truly a brave deed," said Wulstan. "But is that all that you know about the Prince?"

"Oh, no, indeed!" replied Turgar. "I have asked everybody questions about him since then, and I have heard ever so many stories. And in them all he is good and just, as well as brave and strong. Mother told me about his going to Rome when he was only five years old, and of how much the Pope liked him—and that he said he would some day be King."

Turgar was quite breathless when he finished. His father looked into his flushed face and smiled, but the smile was a very tender one. "And so Alfred is your Prince and your hero," he said. "Well, Turgar, you could not find a worthier model. I truly wish that you might see him, and I hope that some day you may."

Then Wulstan went in search of Gyneth, that they might complete their plans for an early start in the morning.

When the party left on the following day no one was quite so happy as Turgar himself, for it had been decided that he should accompany his father and mother as far as the castle, and then return with the escort of soldiers and servants, under the special care of Acca, and a stern young warrior named Algar.

In his heart Turgar hoped that he might by some chance see the Prince, but Gyneth assured him that this was altogether unlikely.

It was a gay procession that started out. They were mounted upon horses wearing rich trappings, while other horses were laden with costly wedding gifts.

For many weeks Gyneth and her maidens had been busily at work weaving and embroidering rich garments and furnishings, while the goldsmith had been equally busy fashioning curious jeweled clasps and bracelets and cups.

When, after several hours of riding, the party reached the castle, the gifts were taken from the packs and carried by the servants into one of the great rooms which had been set aside to receive them.

Then Wulstan and Gyneth bade Turgar good-bye, and gave special charge to Acca and Algar regarding him.

Turgar looked longingly back as he rode away, for although the journey had been full of interest, and the sight of the castle with all its bustling activities had aroused his enthusiasm, his dearest hope—cherished in spite of his mother's words—had not been realized, for he had not seen his Prince.

As they rode along, the men of the company, relieved of the restraint which they felt when in the presence of Wulstan and Withgar, began an eager discussion of the scenes at the castle. They joked and laughed, and even the horses seemed to feel the relaxation of their riders. Turgar rode between Acca and Algar where the width of the road would permit, and listened keenly to the conversation of the men.

The leader of the party was riding some little distance in advance. As he came to an abrupt turn in the road, an arrow shot swiftly across the way, so close to his horse's head that the animal gave a sudden plunge, wheeled about, unseating his rider by the quick and unexpected movement, and galloped madly back among the other horses.

In a moment all was confusion. The horses and many

of the men became panic stricken. Of course the first thought of all was "the Danes!"

In an instant Algar's voice arose in stern command, but although there were soldiers in the company, there were untrained thralls as well, and these lost all control of their plunging horses as well as of themselves.

There was a moment of wild confusion. One of the frightened animals reared, struck the horse upon which Turgar was mounted with his hoofs, and, before Algar or Acca saw what had happened, Turgar was being borne down the road at breakneck speed. At the bend of the road the horse reared, then plunged, and Turgar was thrown in a crumpled heap in the dust.

Algar and Acca followed swiftly, but before they could reach him a strange rider dashed from the side of the road, slipped from his horse, and lifted Turgar's head upon his arm.

"I crave your pardon," he said, as Algar and Acca came up. "I saw a buck in yonder thicket, and sent an arrow after it, not knowing of your approach."

In an instant the two men were beside him in the road, while the men of the company, relieved from their fear of the Danes, were succeeding in quieting the horses, and getting themselves into more orderly array.

Algar's face was dark with rage at the conduct of his

band, which had resulted in such an accident, and been witnessed by the man who now held Turgar's head upon his arm. For this stranger was no stranger to Algar, the soldier; and as the latter leaped from his horse beside him, he gravely saluted as he said: "Your Honor, Prince Alfred!"

But what of Turgar? Stunned by the fall, he lay for a moment wholly unconscious, but as Algar uttered these words it was as though a magic potion had been given him. His eyes opened, and he looked long and earnestly into the face bent above his own.

"Prince Alfred?" he repeated questioningly. "Yes, my boy," was the answer, "I am Prince Alfred."

A sudden flood of color came back into Turgar's face as he raised himself, saluted, and said, still half wonderingly, "My Prince; my hero!"

At these words the eyes of the young prince shone with pleasure, and then he helped Turgar to his feet. Fortunately there were no bones broken, though it had been a bad throw, and in a few moments Turgar declared himself well able to mount and continue his journey.

Algar, muttering imprecations upon his own head for the accident, assisted him to mount, and then Prince Alfred offered Turgar his hand. He blamed himself heartily for the accident and ended by saying, "Some day,

He Looked Long And Earnestly Into
The Face Bent Above His Own.

Turgar, I shall hope to see you again, and then I will try to make amends for this."

But Turgar, with shining eyes, replied, "I trust that I may some day be able to serve you, my Prince."

As they resumed their journey, Algar on one hand and Acca upon the other, Turgar quite forgot the fright and the hurt, for both were crowded out by the joy of having seen and spoken with "his Prince."

CHAPTER IV

A Royal Saxon Wedding

It was several days later when Wulstan and Gyneth returned from the wedding feast.

Prince Alfred had sought out Wulstan at the castle and told him of the accident to Turgar, taking upon himself even more than his share of the blame, but reassuring him as to any serious injury to the lad. Wulstan had therefore had several days in which to let his indignation at the conduct of his men cool, and it is probably well for them that he had.

When, upon their return, he and Gyneth questioned Turgar, the latter exclaimed, "Oh, I was so glad it happened, because if it had not, I would not have seen my Prince." And so, with a laugh, Wulstan let the matter drop.

"Mother," said Turgar the next day, "please tell me all about the wedding. Is Elswitha nice?"

"She seems pike a sweet, sensible girl," answered Gyneth, "and I am sure she is very fond of your Prince."

"Please tell me all about it," repeated Turgar, stretching himself upon the rug before the fire, and looking up into his mother's face. "You see," he added, "I do not know how people are wedded at all, or what they do."

"Well," replied Gyneth with a smile, "I will describe the wedding to you as well as I can. In the first place, Alfred and a company of his friends rode away many miles to the home of Elswitha. He and his company were dressed in their most splendid armor, and they made an imposing company. The old Saxon custom required that they go armed, because in those remote days brides were sometimes carried away from their homes by force, and often there would be a battle with the followers of some other suitor. Those days have passed, but in our own times it is equally necessary for the men to go armed on account of the presence of the Danes in our land; for no one knows when there may be an attack from them.

"But nothing of this kind occurred to Prince Alfred, and he and his company had returned the day before we reached the castle. They brought with them Elswitha and her father, two of her brothers, and a group of young maidens who were to act as her attendants.

"The wedding occurred the day after we arrived, in the church which belongs to the castle. Alfred and Elswitha were dressed in royal garments, heavy with gold embroidery and sparkling with jewels. Each wore a crown of flowers, and the church was decorated with blossoms of many sorts.

"As they stood before the altar, Alfred promised to care for Elswitha as his dearest treasure as long as he lived, and then Elswitha's father gave his consent to their being made man and wife. Then the priest read the wedding service of the church, and gave them his blessing."

"Was that all?" asked Turgar.

"That was all of the wedding ceremony," replied Gyneth, "but after that came the wedding feast, and that lasted very much longer.

"We all went from the church to the castle, and there we took part in a great banquet, where every imaginable kind of food was served. There were singers and harpists and minstrels to entertain us. They sang the old ballads of kings and conquests, and then they sang a group of songs which had been newly written in honor of Alfred's brave deeds and noble courage. And they sang, too, of Elswitha's high birth and gentle courtesy.

"The feasting and song lasted all night and far into the next day, and then Alfred and his bride rode away to their own home."

"Did they have many gifts?" asked Turgar, as his mother finished, for he had been greatly interested in the work of his mother and the goldsmith in the days preceding the wedding.

"Wagon loads of them," answered Gyneth. "When they started away it looked like a triumphal procession. We all stood in the castle grounds and waved our scarfs and banners till they were out of sight."

"What sort of presents were there?" persisted Turgar, for no detail of this wonderful wedding was to be overlooked.

"There were beautiful chains and clasps and rings, made from gold and silver and precious stones," replied Gyneth. "There were dishes of gold and of silver, cups with jeweled edges, tapestries and hangings of the richest embroidery, and furniture with wonderful carving upon it. I am sure all the most skilled workmen of the land must have been busy for many months to produce the wonderful things that were given."

"Oh, I am glad!" exclaimed Turgar. "I wish I knew some of the songs that the minstrels sang—the new songs that told about the Prince."

"Perhaps Withgar will remember them," Gyneth replied. "He sings well, and would be apt to remember the words. I am sure he will be glad to teach them to you when he returns."

"But when will Withgar come back?" asked Turgar.

"He went with the singers and musicians and friends who accompanied Alfred and Elswitha to their home."

"Oh, then when he comes he will be sure to know the new songs," cried Turgar happily, and he ran out to the yard, where he found Acca feeding the dogs.

"Oh, Acca," he cried, "Mother has just been telling me all about the wedding and the feasting, and the presents. It must have been a wonderful time, and I can shut my eyes and imagine it all, for now, you see, I know just how the Prince looks."

Poor Acca's face flushed deeply, as it did every time he was reminded of the accident to Turgar, but the lad was too intent to notice. "Oh," Turgar added, "I would not have missed seeing him for anything! I don't believe I would have minded if the fall had broken my leg."

"Bless you!" said Acca fervently. "It is some comfort to hear you say that."

CHAPTER V

LEAVING HOME

Long before the time of our story the Saxons had given up the worship of Thor and of Odin, and had accepted the Christian religion; but in those days all the Christians in England were Romanists, and their teachers were bishops and priests.

There were those among the older or the more ignorant of the people who still clung to the old Norse religion with its many gods and heroes; but even they were in a sad state of doubt when they realized that this was the religion of the hated Danes, whom they called savages and barbarians.

The monasteries and abbeys of Saxon England were the seats of learning. The monks could read both Saxon and Latin, and when any man determined to learn to read and to write he entered a monastery as a pupil. Those who intended to devote their lives to the service of the church became priests; but others went to the monastery to study for a time only, expecting to take their place again in the world when their services were needed by the King, or for private duties. In this way the monasteries took the place of schools; indeed, they were the only schools the Saxons had.

Most of the people, however, were too busy fighting, or getting ready to fight the Danes, to think or care much whether they could read or write. If it were necessary for them to sign a document, some priest could write the name for them and beneath that they could place their mark, which answered the same purpose. Few even of the kings, up to this time, could write their own names.

Wulstan and Gyneth had noticed Turgar's eagerness to learn, and his interest in all the historical tales that were told him, and they had at length decided to place him in an abbey where he could study under the monks, and learn at least how to read and to write.

When the news was told to Turgar he was at first quite overwhelmed. He was delighted at the prospect of knowing for himself how to read, and yet he wondered how, with all his restlessness and love of activity, he could ever adapt himself to the quiet life of a monastery.

"They will not require too much of you, my son," said Wulstan, when Turgar spoke of this. "The monks are men like ourselves, and some of them have been active warriors. They will give you the freedom that you need, if you win their approval. And you are not going with the idea of becoming a priest, but only as a pupil."

So Turgar was reassured, and when the time came for him to accompany his father he was very happy, except for the sorrow of parting from his mother.

Withgar rode with them, and a body-guard followed, made up of soldiers and servants, or thralls. It was scarcely safe even for two or three to venture off to a distance alone, since they might be overtaken by a party of marauding Danes at any time. No outrages had been committed recently, but the Saxons never knew when there might be a raid.

The Saxons had become a quiet people, and they had little love for fighting; but they were often forced to fight in order to protect their homes and those that they loved.

Nothing was sacred to the wild, fierce Danes. They burned houses and churches, they tortured and killed not only men, but women and children, till men shuddered to hear of their cruel and blood-thirsty deeds. They carried away the treasures of homes which they plundered, and then set fire to the buildings. The Saxons had repeatedly defeated them in battle, but new hordes kept coming from the north until, to the more thoughtful of the thanes, the struggle began to seem endless.

"Tell me more about Crowland, Father," said Turgar, as they rode along a quiet road—for Crowland was the name of the abbey in which he was to study.

"Crowland Abbey lies between two rivers," replied Wulstan, "and it is a very large stone building. There are several hundred monks living there, and it is one of the greatest abbeys in the land."

"It has had many rich gifts," added Withgar, "and it has great quantities of gold and silver plate, of jeweled robes and vestments. There is one table in the church, used in the service of the altar, which is covered with gold. And there are relics and treasures of priceless worth within its walls."

"Is there any one there that you know?" asked Turgar, struggling against a sudden feeling of homesickness which seized him.

"Oh, yes, indeed," answered his father. "The Abbot Theodore has been my friend from boyhood. He is prior of the abbey, and he will be like a father to you."

"Then there is Friar Joly, whom you are sure to like. He is a warrior as well as a priest, and he can tell you scores of stories such as you like to hear. Besides, he will teach you how to read such stories from books."

"It will all seem very strange," said Turgar, "but I think I shall like it."

"I am sure you will, my son," replied Wulstan. Then he drew rein and pointed some distance ahead. "Do you see the gray turrets yonder between the trees?" he asked, and when Turgar nodded he said, "That is your first view of Crowland Abbey. We will soon be there."

Turgar sat very erect upon his horse. It was the first time he had taken a long journey away from home, and he was filled with conflicting emotions. He would be glad to study, he was quite sure of that, although it was a great mystery, this learning how the strange marks upon a piece of white parchment could say things to you. But they surely could, for a priest who visited at their home had shown him a small volume and had read to him what the marks said.

He wished that he had brought Wulf, his great dog, for he felt just now as though Wulf would be a great comfort after his father and Withgar had gone.

Suddenly he turned to Withgar and said, "I hope you will bring home another boar soon, Withgar. I wanted to go with you hunting some day, but now I shall not have a chance."

"Oh, yes, you will!" replied Withgar. "You will be home again one of these days, and then we will go hunting together. And you may not find life at Crowland as quiet, perhaps, as you think. With so many men and boys here you will have plenty of company."

"Oh, I am going to like it," exclaimed Turgar sturdily, "but don't forget the boar hunt we are going to have together."

CHAPTER VI
The Abbey

The Prior Theodore met Wulstan and his party as they drew rein at the abbey door. He greeted Wulstan warmly, and laid a protecting hand upon the shoulder of Turgar.

"He shall be to me like an own son," he said, looking into Turgar's face approvingly. "It is well for him to study, and in the stress and uncertainty of the times I trust that he will be safer here—though the Danes stop not for the cross," he added in a low voice, speaking more to himself than to his friends.

At the earnest invitation of the prior, Wulstan and Withgar remained overnight at the abbey, while the soldiers and thralls of their company made themselves comfortable in the court.

At the call to prayer they all went with the monks to the chapel. The service was in Latin, so none of them understood the words, but the reverent attitude of the monks, and the sweet face and voice of the prior, impressed them strangely, and Turgar felt rather than understood the contrast between the atmosphere of the monastery and that of the turbulent, restless life outside.

He enjoyed the singing of the monks, accompanied by the playing of pipes. The singing was different from any that he had heard. He was accustomed to the free, bold songs of Withgar and his friends when they sang in praise of great battles, or in honor of some brave warrior. Often, too, they sang the older Saxon songs of the heroes of Asgard, of the Viking ships and their dauntless crews; although such songs were beginning to be looked upon with disfavor by those who were devoted to the church. But Turgar loved the wild freedom of their music, and when he heard such singing he often exclaimed, half in fun and yet half in earnest, "The blood of the Sea Kings runs wild in my veins,"—for was it not literally true, although he no longer worshiped the mighty Thor?

But he liked, too, this strangely monotonous music of the monks, this chanting of psalms, for the voices of the men rolled forth with a solemn musical cadence that rose and fell, and seemed to bear him along with it into unknown spaces.

The music ceased, the prior arose and stretched forth his hands in benediction, and Turgar reverently bowed his head, though the Latin words held no meaning for his ears.

After the service, Wulstan and his sons were shown through the chapel and the abbey by the priest Joly, whom the prior summoned.

All the rich treasures of the abbey were displayed, and Turgar wondered at the enormous wealth, the priceless gifts, which had been brought or sent to the monastery by devoted Catholics of the land. There were gold and silver vessels for the service of the chapel; the vestments for the priests were richly embroidered and heavy with fringes of gold. There were robes of the most costly materials, and golden chains, and candlesticks, and crosses, the latter several feet in height.

It was a new and wonderful sight to Turgar, and even to Wulstan and Withgar, for although this was not their first visit to a monastery, the Abbey of Crowland was unusually rich in treasures.

But, as they went from one wonder to another, Turgar watched the face of the monk Joly quite as much as he did the golden candle-sticks, or the rich robes. There was something about this priest which attracted and fascinated him. He remembered that Wulstan had said that he was a soldier as well as a priest, and although that seems to us a strange combination, the conditions in Saxon England were such that even the priests were at times called upon to fight, and Friar Joly had been a leader of the monks in more than one scrimmage upon the field of battle. And so it was to this soldier-priest that Turgar was especially drawn, for he seemed to him to combine the elements of his own old life and the new one upon which he was just entering.

He felt sure that he would find a father in the Prior Theodore, and he knew already that it would be easy to love him; but in Friar Joly he saw a companion and friend whom he could meet upon a more familiar level.

And the monk responded to the boy's eager interest, and told many strange stories connected with the various gifts, and with the people who had bestowed them.

"You may be interested in the story of this cup," he said, as he handed a heavy golden goblet to Wulstan. "It has long been in the abbey, but it is said to have belonged at one time to King Arthur who, with his Knights of the Round Table, fought so valiantly against our Saxon forefathers. He was a King of whom the Britons had a right to be proud, for he was strong, and daring, and powerful. He fought giants and wild beasts single-handed and overcame them. And he was kind and chivalrous, as well as strong, and his Knights loved him, and would have died for him."

"And yet he was not a Saxon?" asked Turgar in surprise, for the story was a new one to him.

"No, indeed," replied the friar, with a laugh. "He probably had the same feeling toward the Saxons that we now have toward the Danes."

Turgar's eyes opened wide.

"The early Saxons, you remember," continued the friar, "came from much the same stock that the Danes do. They were wild and fierce rovers of the sea, and they fought the Britons, over whom King Arthur ruled, much as the Danes fight us."

Even Withgar was surprised at such a statement as this.

"It is quite true," said Friar Joly. "We worshiped Thor and Woden, as you know some of our people do to this day." The older men nodded in assent.

"But when our forefathers had overcome the Britons," he continued, "they gave up the sea and settled down to till the soil and become permanent residents of the land. That helped to change their character and habits, but the one thing that changed them most completely was their giving up the worship of heathen gods and accepting Christianity. The religion of Christ has in it no place for cruelty or lust or revenge, even though men are forced sometimes to fight for the protection of their homes, their families, or the church."

Friar Joly's stories had awakened the keenest interest on the part of Turgar, and had aroused in him a great desire to read, and so to learn for himself the early history of his land and his people. He wanted to know more about this King Arthur and his Knights. And so when the time came for Wulstan and Withgar to return, he was quite willing to remain at the abbey, for with Friar Joly as a companion he felt sure that the days would not be dull.

CHAPTER VII

From Abbey to Army

Nearly two years had passed since Turgar had come to Crowland Abbey.

At first the life had seemed very quiet to him, but he became deeply interested in his studies, he loved the Prior Theodore devotedly, and his admiration for Friar Joly knew no bounds.

He had learned to read the Saxon language, and was making good progress with his Latin.

Practically all the books in the monastery were written in Latin, but the monks devoted much of their time to translating these into Saxon and making copies of them in their own tongue. All books of that time were really manuscripts written by hand upon parchment, and the copying of a single book took many, many weeks. The monks tried to make their work as perfect as possible, and the letters of titles, or at the beginning of chapters or paragraphs, were often illuminated in rich colors. Sometimes these illuminated letters were embellished with very small heads, sometimes with landscapes, or

39

figures or flowers. Gold was used with the rich colors, and the work was often very beautiful.

This hand process of making books, as well as their great scarcity, gave to each one a value which we of to-day can scarcely comprehend. A book was one of the rarest gifts that one friend could give to another, and only the nobles and families of great wealth had so much as one.

After Turgar had learned to read there were not many books in the monastery which were of any use to him, since only those that had been translated into Saxon had any meaning for him. But these few he read as often as possible, and from them and the tales told him by the monks he gained a very good idea of the history of his country and the deeds of his forefathers.

The works on theology he found rather hard to understand, but he read eagerly the poems and psalms, and found much of interest in the books of the law. The book that he loved best of all, however, was the book of psalms, which seemed to him to contain all the beautiful thoughts of the world.

He had not been long in the monastery when his friend, the good Joly, permitted him to use some of his paints and brushes, for no one in all the monastery could do more beautiful illuminating than the soldier-priest.

THE GOOD *JOLY* PERMITTED HIM TO USE
SOME OF HIS PAINTS AND BRUSHES.

Turgar was delighted. Painting was a wholly new occupation to him, but he was fascinated by it, even though his first efforts were poor and crude. In spite of this fact, Friar Joly saw that the lad had a latent talent, and he encouraged him to keep on. Within a few weeks Turgar was illuminating letters with greater skill and taste than some of the monks had ever been able to do.

The various studies, and the daily services in the chapel, together with the hours given to recreation, filled Turgar's days so full that he had little time for loneliness. There were other boys in the monastery, too, and with them he spent his recreation hours in outdoor games and contests that developed his physical strength. Their sports consisted in games of ball, discus throwing, and foot races.

Turgar was a favorite with all. He was not only studious, which pleased the monks, but he was strong, athletic, and full of a fine courage that made him a leader among the boys.

One day as Turgar sat beside Friar Joly, bending over a Latin manuscript and trying to translate some of its unfamiliar phrases, they heard a sound of rapid hoof beats, and then some one pounded heavily upon the outer door.

In a moment all work within the monastery ceased.

Friar Joly slipped the precious book back within its case, and all waited with suspended breath.

The prior answered the summons in person. A little later he returned, his face set and stern, and very white.

"The Danes are to the north of us," he said. "King Ethelred is sorely pressed, and has need of reinforcements."

Instantly the sober band of monks was transformed.

"I beg of you, give me a band of men to lead out!" cried Friar Joly. And a chorus of voices shouted, "Take me! Take me!"

In less than an hour's time there issued from the monastery gates an orderly company of soldiers, although still clad in the garb of monks. Friar Joly was in command.

Turgar's blood tingled as he saw them march away, and his heart beat fast. He would have been glad to form one of the band under the leadership of his beloved friar, for he felt that it would be a glorious thing to help even a little in battling against the cruel Danes.

"Oh, I wish I were a few years older!" he exclaimed to Heribert, one of his boy friends. "Nothing could hold me back then."

"Indeed," answered Heribert, "it would be much easier to go than to stay. I wonder how near the Danes are to Crowland."

But their conversation was interrupted by the bell calling them to prayer in the chapel.

The following days passed slowly to the thirty or forty inmates of the abbey. Their thoughts were with their comrades rather than upon parchments or the singing of psalms. They well knew that if conditions had not been desperate with the army of King Ethelred, he would not have asked for reinforcements from the abbey. But there were no means of communication. They could only wait and hope.

In the midst of his anxiety the good Prior Theodore did not forget Turgar, for he knew how greatly the lad would miss his friend, Friar Joly, and how distressed he would be regarding him.

Theodore had well kept his promise to Wulstan, that Turgar should be to him as his own son. He truly loved the lad, and his love was warmly returned.

On the second morning following the departure of the monks he sought Turgar out. "Come," he said, "I will hear your lesson in Latin to-day. Bring me your book."

Turgar took the manuscript to the prior and began to read. But try as he would to keep his mind upon his lesson, he made sad work of it.

"I do not always read so badly," he said at length, looking up into the prior's face. But he saw at once that the prior had not heard either his bad Latin or his apology for it. The eyes of Theodore were filled with a look of anxious dread, and it was evident that his thoughts were many leagues away.

With a start he came to himself, as he felt Turgar's gaze upon him. He took the manuscript and replaced it in its case. Then he laid his hand upon Turgar's shoulder with an affectionate clasp, and with a gentle smile he said, "We will try it again another day."

But little the kind old prior dreamed what another day would bring to his beloved abbey.

CHAPTER VIII
THE RAID

It was late in the evening. The monks were assembled once more in the little chapel to engage in prayer. The psalms had been chanted to the accompaniment of the pipes, and Theodore and the diminished company of monks had knelt, when suddenly there came a pounding upon the door. It was burst open, and three men, cut and bleeding and weary, staggered over the threshold.

"May the Lord have mercy!" cried Theodore, as he rose and hurried down the chapel aisle.

The monks scrambled to their feet, they cried out in dismay, and then they crowded about the three men.

Turgar mounted a bench that he might see them more plainly,—then he covered his face in horror. One was Friar Joly, but so pale and haggard that he hardly knew him, and with a cut across his face that told how desperately near he had come to death.

But what was it that the men were saying?

"Fly! Fly! The Danes are close at hand! They will soon be upon us. They have learned of the rich treasures of

Crowland, and they care nothing for the cross. Gold and booty are what they are after, and they hate the Christ, for they worship Woden. We are all that remain of the two hundred who marched away from Crowland!"

There was little time for lament. "What shall we do?" was the one question asked.

Weary and weak as he was, Joly was the one to suggest a plan of action, and the prior at once gave commands to carry it out.

"A boat is at the nearest point on the river," he said. "It is dark, but you know the way, and it is close by. Take all the treasures that can be carried and put them in the boat."

Swiftly, and as silently as possible, all the inmates of the monastery set to work. Gold and silver, jeweled ornaments, and embroidered fabrics were carried to the river. The golden cup which Friar Joly had said once belonged to King Arthur was put into Turgar's hand, and with his other he caught up a massive silver candlestick and bore them swiftly to the boat. Heribert ran with him, carrying two jeweled cups which had been standing before the altar.

"I know all the woods and paths about here," Heribert said in an undertone, as they hurried back for other treasure. "My home is not far away, and I have always hunted and trapped small game. Keep with me if you can, should the Danes come."

Presently the voice of Theodore rang out. "Hear me!" he called. "If any treasure is left we will conceal it afterward in the woods, or by dropping it into the water of the well. The boat must be taken down the river to the hermitage of Gyrth. He knows all the secret places, and will conceal both men and treasure. I will remain here with the older men and some of the boys. We could not defend ourselves against the Danish horde even if all were to stay. If we attempt no defense we may be spared."

A cry of protest went up from all the monks. They could not leave the prior without defense! They would not save themselves and leave him unprotected!

But Theodore was adamant. The younger men and treasures must be saved for the future good of the church. If he must, he would gladly give his life; but he could not leave his abbey. His very defencelessness would save him.

The monks protested, plead, rebelled; but the prior was firm, and as their superior he commanded that they obey.

Slowly and sadly the strong men of the abbey filed down to the river-bank, boarded the boats, and glided away down the river. The three who had returned weary and bleeding were taken with them, although Friar Joly had resisted with all his remaining strength, and only the solemn command of the prior had reduced him to submission.

"The church and the country have need of you. Go!" And Friar Joly bowed his head and was led away.

"Of what use can we be?" whispered Heribert, with white lips, to Turgar.

The prior, a few old men, and four or five boys were all that were left in defense of Crowland.

"Come," said Heribert, laying hold upon Turgar's tunic. "I know all the ways of the woods hereabout. We can slip away unseen."

The Danes were coming. He had not even a knife with which to defend himself. He could be of no use to any one. These were the thoughts that went like a series of lightning flashes through Turgar's mind. Then he looked toward the altar where the Prior Theodore knelt.

In an instant Turgar's head was thrown back. "Go, if you will," he cried. And then, in a softer tone, he continued: "It is not in my heart to blame you; but whether I can help him or not, I shall not desert my prior."

A moment later Heribert had gone.

A few treasures and relics had been left behind or dropped in the hurry of departure, and those who remained busied themselves in carrying these to the well and dropping them into the water. Two or three forgotten manuscripts were hastily buried at the foot of a shattered oak.

Daylight was beginning to break, and the feeling of relief, which always comes with the approach of light, was stealing over the little group in the abbey when they heard a far-away shout, then another. Then came a chorus of horrid yells, the tramp of many feet.

The Danes were descending upon Crowland.

Turgar sprang to the side of the prior, not for protection, but—if there were a possibility of such a thing—to protect; and with blazing eyes he stood there.

"Save yourself, if you can," said Theodore. "Your country has need of such as you."

The prior had thought to speak to the leader of the Danes and throw his helpless band upon his mercy. But there was no time for speech or protestation. The merciless Danes poured into the building, searched in vain for the treasure they had hoped to find in such abundance, and in their frenzied anger at being thwarted, turned upon the little band and thrust them through with their spears.

Turgar, standing with clenched hands beside the prior, saw him stricken, and, tearing aside his own tunic, he took a step forward with bared breast and blazing eyes, saying: "You have killed my prior; kill me, too."

The hand of the Dane was already raised to thrust, but

He Took A Step Forward With Bared Breast.

for an instant he paused and looked into the handsome, fearless face of the boy.

His arm dropped. "You are brave enough to be a Dane," he said, and with a quick motion he drew him beneath his own mantle.

"Follow me," he said, "wherever I go."

A moment later the Dane drew him to one side, stripped off his torn tunic and threw about him a Danish cloak. "Keep close to me," he repeated. "I am Count Sidroc. I will save you, and make you a Dane."

At the words, "I will make you a Dane," Turgar was about to tear off the cloak and bare himself once more for a thrust, but at the instant he remembered the words of his prior—the last command which he could ever give—"Save yourself, if you can. Your country has need of such as you."

CHAPTER IX
Turgar's Escape

Turgar, sick at heart, and full of wrath, nevertheless kept close to Count Sidroc.

From one part of the abbey to another the Danes went, searching for the treasures they believed were hidden. Finding little of value, their wrath knew no bounds, for they well knew that not an abbey in the country was reputed to hold as great treasure as Crowland.

"To the tombs, then!" cried the leader. "No doubt there is treasure there."

At this the men grasped their weapons and used them to beat, and pry, and hammer, until they had broken open the tombs of the monastery, and rifled them of such ornaments and treasures as had been buried there.

Turgar reeled with sickening horror at the scene.

"Who is this?" cried one of the Danes, stopping for a moment in his work to look into Turgar's face. He raised his weapon; then he hesitated for a moment as he noted the Danish cloak.

At that moment Sidroc wheeled about. "Hold!" he shouted. "He is a Dane, and my attendant."

The fellow muttered a word of apology, though he still looked with unconvinced eyes at Turgar. But, in another moment, he turned to snatch up a jeweled bracelet which had been stolen from one of the tombs and dropped by the plunderer, and so the boy was forgotten.

At last the marauding band was convinced that they had found all that there was of value, and prepared to leave. But their lust for cruelty and revenge was not yet satisfied. Piling together the bodies of the slain monks, they set fire to the monastery and marched away to the sound of the crackling flames.

Turgar had hoped that he might at the last slip away from Sidroc and hide, but Sidroc seemed never to forget him for a moment.

As he marched away with the hated Danes and looked back at the burning abbey his heart cried out, "Oh, my prior! Your fate is far happier than mine."

From Crowland the Danes marched to another abbey, which was also famed for its treasure, and there they repeated their terrifying attack. The inmates here had not been warned in advance, and the marauders were richly rewarded. They carried away great stores of gold and silver, rich vestments and robes, and these they loaded into wagons.

When they at last marched away, Count Sidroc was placed in charge of the rear wagon, into which the heaviest and richest of the plunder had been piled.

Across the marshes and through the forest roads they marched, the men singing wild snatches of songs of the Northland, stopping now and then to put their shoulder to a wagon which was mired, or to repair a broken harness which had given way under the tugging of the horses, for the roads were rough and stony in places, and soft and miry in others.

The men seemed never to tire, and to Turgar, unused to traveling long distances on foot, the way seemed endless. But he clenched his fists and kept up, for he would not prove less hardy than these hated Danes—though he had had no food that day.

At length the line of march was halted long enough to eat a hasty meal, and Count Sidroc saw that Turgar was given his full share, so that when they again went on he felt much stronger and able to think more clearly.

Presently there was a great shouting ahead, and once more they stopped. Word was sent back that those in advance were crossing a stream, and that the bottom was rocky and the water deep. The men could wade or swim, but it was difficult to get the horses and wagons across.

Slowly the lines moved forward, until just as dusk began to creep upon them the wagon under Sidroc's care, the last of the line, reached the edge of the stream.

"We must hasten on or night will overtake us before we reach our boats," said Sidroc to the driver, who urged his horses forward.

Then, turning to a companion, Sidroc added, "The boats are just beyond the point of land which separates this troublesome stream from the main river. We must get this booty on board our ships to-night. It is too valuable to run any risk of losing."

"You are right," his companion answered. "The prating priests cheated us at Crowland, or we would have had twice as much."

The wagon was now in the stream, and the men were just entering the water when they heard a sudden bump, and then a sound of grinding and wrenching, and the breaking of heavy wood.

Sidroc sprang forward with a great oath and splashed through the water. His companion followed. Turgar, who was just entering the water at Sidroc's side, looked up just in time to see the wagon lurch and throw the driver into the stream.

In a moment all was confusion. One of the wagon wheels had struck a boulder and been wrenched off, breaking the heavy axle. The men shouted and called to those ahead, and the men nearest came back to help. They swarmed into the water, trying to prop the wagon so that its treasure should not be lost in the stream. Each man was intent on trying to avert a worse disaster to the precious load. Sidroc was in command, floundering here and there in the water, shouting orders, and hurrying the men, for darkness was settling down upon them.

"Now is my time," muttered Turgar under his breath.

He ran along the edge of the water as others were doing in their search for stones and timber with which to prop up the broken wagon. A little farther up the stream a great branch of a tree hung almost to the water's edge. Turgar reached it and hid behind its shelter for a moment to see whether his action had been noticed. But no one had thought of the boy in the excitement and turmoil.

Seeing this, he turned, and, still sheltered from sight by the branch, clambered up the bank and slipped in among the trees. Then he began to run, back, back, anywhere, away from the cruel Danes.

He knew nothing of the country he was in. He dared not make his way back to the road. It was rapidly growing dark.

He ran on and on, with nothing to guide his course except that as he ran the noise and shouting of the Danes grew less and less distinct, until at last he could hear it no more.

Exhausted, he at last dropped to the ground, weary, hungry, and footsore, and somewhat sheltered by the trunk of a great tree, he laid his head upon a hummock of earth and fell asleep.

CHAPTER X
HERIBERT

"Turgar! Turgar!" The name was spoken softly but insistently. The lad who called waited a moment. Then he took hold of the Danish cloak and pulled it a bit as he again called softly, "Turgar!"

Slowly Turgar's eyes opened, and he looked up—into the face of Heribert. "Why—" he began slowly, too dazed for the moment to realize where he was or what had happened. Then he leaped to his feet.

"Heribert!" he cried. "Where am I? Was it all a terrible dream? Tell me, Heribert! How came you here, or are all the horrors a part of my dream?"

"Softly," whispered Heribert, placing his hand upon Turgar's lips; and then he added, "No, Turgar, the horrors were all too real. But I told you that I knew the woods and all the country hereabout, and after I had run away I was ashamed, and I did not go far. I climbed up into a tree, high up, and I pulled the branches close about me, so that I was sure I could not be seen, and then I watched. Oh, Turgar, I know what followed! I heard them in the chapel, murdering, and chopping and hewing at the tombs and the altar. I thought you all had been killed. I saw the smoke come curling over the abbey walls and through the windows, and I saw the Danes march away. And then, Turgar, I saw a boy in a Danish cloak amongst them, and I looked sharp and saw that it was you. Oh, Turgar, I cannot tell you how I felt then, for I knew that that was worse than death.

"When the Danes had gone far enough so that I dared, I climbed down from the tree. I could not save the abbey from the flames, though I tried; then I thought I would try to save you.

"I had no plan, but I followed, away off to one side through the woods. The voices of the Danes guided me, and I knew the road they had taken. I saw them reach the second abbey, and I watched them load their wagons with the treasure they had stolen. Then again I followed them, till at last they came to the ford where the water was high and covered the rocks. Under cover of the darkness I drew nearer, and then I heard the tumult, and learned what had happened to one of the wagons. Then, oh, Turgar, a wonderful thought came to me!

"I went farther down the stream and swam across, and I listened on the farther side and learned that the Danes had concluded to spend the night at the river, for they feared to leave the treasure that was in the broken wagon. I was near enough in the darkness to hear them talk, and I learned just where their ships were at anchor—the ships upon which they intended to sail away with the treasure they had stolen. They were just across a strip of land, for there is the river. And I knew exactly, then, where I was. Oh, I could have shouted, but I dared not!

"I ran as fast as I could in the darkness until I came to the river, and there lay the Danish fleet. Five boats in all.

"Turgar!" cried Heribert, gripping his companion's arm, "I took my knife from my belt, placed it between my teeth, and swam out to where the boats were moored, and I cut the ropes that held them, one by one. I feared that there would be Danes on board, but I saw no one, and as I cut the ropes the ships began floating away with the current, toward the sea."

As Heribert finished he sank down upon the ground, and Turgar was frightened, for he thought that Heribert had fainted.

"Heribert!" he called, as softly and intently as Heribert had called his own name a few moments before.

Heribert opened his eyes and sat up. "This is no time to collapse," he said. "There is still work ahead of us."

Turgar's eyes were gleaming. "And the Danish ships are gone!" he cried.

"Gone!" answered Heribert. "I know not how far, of course, but so long as I could see them the current carried them free of the banks, and the sea was not far distant."

"And how did you get back? How did you find me?" asked Turgar, scarcely able to breathe for excitement over Heribert's tale.

"That was an accident," replied Heribert, "although I am sure our good prior would not put it so. He would have said it was the providence of God. But I ran back because I wanted to arouse Oswyn the Saxon, and tell him of the plight of the Danes. Perhaps he could yet gather enough men to attack them and get back the treasure that was stolen. And then, on my way back, just as the dawn broke, I saw what looked like a Danish cloak at the foot of a tree, and I stooped over it—and I saw your face. Oh, Turgar, I never can tell you how thankful I am that you escaped. How did you manage it?"

"They were all so busy with the broken wagon and the danger to the stolen treasure that they forgot me. I saw my chance and slipped away under cover of the darkness. But it was nothing—nothing, to what you did!"

"Ah!" said Heribert sorrowfully, "but you stayed and faced death, while I ran away."

"Don't, Heribert, don't!" cried Turgar. "You have more

than made up for that. But come, you were on the way to the home of Oswyn. Can we not go on together?"

"Yes," said Heribert, "and we must hasten, for the Saxons must attack the Danes before they leave the ford, for now their arms are laid aside while they work."

"Come then," said Turgar, springing to his feet.

"It is not far," said Heribert.

Cautiously, yet as rapidly as possible, the two boys ran on, Heribert in the lead, for he seemed to find his way through the woods and marshes as a deer finds its way to water.

Once they stopped to gather a handful of wild berries, for neither one had tasted food for many hours, and they were weak and faint. Yet still they ran on.

At another time Heribert ran to one side to pull a strange looking plant. Rubbing the dirt from Its long tuberous root with his tunic, he broke it in half and handed one piece to Turgar. "Eat it," he said, it will strengthen you." And, eating the root as they went, they ran on.

They kept watch to right and to left, for they feared that straggling Danes might have stayed behind to search for further booty, but they saw no one.

Presently Heribert pointed ahead, and Turgar saw that they were approaching a cluster of buildings.

"That is the home of Oswyn," said Heribert, and in a

few moments they staggered up to the door and pounded upon it with all their remaining strength.

When Oswyn answered the summons he was amazed to see upon his threshold two haggard, wild-eyed boys, one in a ragged, dirty tunic, the other in a crumpled Danish cloak.

"What means this?" he asked.

"Oh, Oswyn," cried Heribert, "I am Heribert, and this is Turgar. We are from the monastery at Crowland which the Danes have burned. Listen to my story; call your men; give us food and drink!"

The members of Oswyn's household gathered quickly about. Oswyn insisted upon each boy's drinking a glass of mead before they told their tale, and then all listened with breathless interest while they were told of the horrors of the raid upon Crowland and the second abbey, and then of the present plight of the Danes.

Hurriedly Oswyn sent out messengers and gathered together a band of armed men. The Saxons of those days were always prepared for battle, and in an incredibly short space of time they were upon the way.

Turgar and Heribert, strengthened by a hearty meal, accompanied them, to direct them by the shortest route back to the ford.

CHAPTER XI

A Reward and a Victory

The band of well-armed men had reached the road which led to the ford, not far distant, when Oswyn turned to the boys.

"You must not go farther," he said. "You have no weapons, no armor, and the fight is likely to be a bitter one." Then, seeing the deep disappointment in their faces, he added: "You have done your part and done it well. When you are grown you will be among the bravest and truest of the King's men. Save yourselves for that." Then he rode away.

Instantly the words of his beloved prior came back to Turgar's mind. "Save yourself, if you can. The country has need of such as you." And though it was a great disappointment to see the men ride forward while they remained behind, the boys knew there was nothing for them to do but obey.

"Let us wait here," said Turgar. "I must learn how the battle goes. Oh, what would I not give to see the Danes when they discover that their ships are gone!"

"Our Saxons are bound to defeat them, if they are still at the ford. Then, I imagine, the Danes will retreat, thinking to get away on their ships. And the ships will be gone!" Turgar's eyes shone as he pictured this hoped-for outcome of the battle, and Heribert laughed aloud as he listened.

Then suddenly Turgar spoke again. "Heribert," he exclaimed, "I have an idea! The band of monks who left the abbey and took the treasure in their boat must still be with the hermit, Gyrth. Friar Joly is with them. Could we not tell them? They would join Oswyn's company. Could you find the hermitage?"

"I know it well," replied Heribert. "Come!"

Once more the boys ran through the woods, their hearts beating high with hope. Could they but send a band of men to reinforce Oswyn's forces they would not feel as though they were merely useless boys, left behind at the approach of danger. "Sometimes boys can help, if they are brave," Turgar said to himself, unconsciously repeating the words he had spoken to his mother after she had told him of the Pope's words regarding his Prince.

Heribert seemed instinctively to know his way, and it was not long before they came to the hermitage. It was so well concealed that Turgar had no thought of its being near until they came directly upon it. "It is no wonder the prior thought it a good place for concealment!" he exclaimed.

In a moment the boys were surrounded by the monks, their familiar friends and companions of the monastery. Hurriedly, but sorrowfully, they told of the destruction of the abbey, and of the death of the prior and of the faithful few who remained with him. Turgar, in a few brief words, recounted his capture and escape, told of Heribert's bold adventure in cutting adrift the Danish ships, and then of Oswyn's company, now on their way to the ford.

It was a breathless account, given in the barest outlines, for their main message was, "Hasten, and join Oswyn's men!"

"Stay with Gyrth and the treasure," commanded Joly, as the monks prepared to ride away. "Those of us who return," he added grimly, "will bring you news of the battle."

He stopped long enough to clasp Turgar's hand, and then Heribert's, and both boys offered a fervent prayer, as they saw him ride away, that he might once more be spared from the Danish sword.

The vast treasures of Crowland had been hastily buried and concealed by the monks as soon as they had reached the hermitage, so the boys felt that it would be easier to follow

Friar Joly's command to remain behind than Oswyn's, for here there were vast treasures for them to guard!

And Gyrth, though a hermit, proved a most companionable man, for he was bound to admire these two boys who were proving themselves so fearless and efficient!

When the monks had gone he asked the boys for their story in detail, and when Turgar told of the cruel massacre in the monastery Gyrth covered his face with his hands. When he again looked up he said, "What a monstrous thing! But our good Prior Theodore has gone to his reward, and his faithful companions with him!"

Then he entertained the boys by telling them of the coming of the monks, and of the hasty burial of the treasure.

In the midst of his recital a step was heard outside the door. Instantly the three sprang to their feet, their hands upon the knives in their belts.

"Friends, I trust!" said a hearty voice, and a man stood in the doorway, his horse's bridle over his arm.

At sight of him Gyrth dropped upon his knee, and motioned to the boys to do the same, but Turgar needed no bidding, for he recognized in the unexpected visitor none other than "his Prince."

"I have ridden on in advance of my men," said Alfred, when he had bidden the three arise, "and by the merest chance I stumbled upon your well-hidden retreat."

Humbly Gyrth invited the Prince to enter, and hastily he set before him some of the food which had been carried from the monastery to the boat.

"You fare well," said the Prince, "and as I have ridden long and hard, your entertainment is most welcome."

"'Tis good fare, Your Honor, but dearly bought," replied Gyrth sadly.

"What mean you?" asked Alfred.

"'Tis from the Abbey of Crowland, Your Honor, which the Danes have just destroyed," answered Gyrth.

"Destroyed! Crowland!" exclaimed Alfred, rising, and involuntarily putting his hand upon his sword.

"Came you not that way?" inquired Gyrth. "It is a terrible tale, but the lads here can tell you of it better than I, Your Honor, for they were witnesses to the attack."

Alfred resumed his seat and looked earnestly at the boys. A puzzled expression came into his eyes as his gaze rested upon Turgar. Then it cleared and he exclaimed, "Are you not the son of Wulstan, and brother of Withgar!"

"Do you remember me, Your Honor?" cried Turgar, and there was a joyous ring to his voice.

"I ought to," answered the Prince, "when I caused you so bad a fall. But you have grown much since then! And were you in the abbey when it was attacked?" he asked. "Tell me all about it."

So, once more, Turgar told in detail all the horrors of the massacre and of the burning of the abbey. He told how the treasure was first carried away, and that it was brought to the hermitage of Gyrth where they now were. And then he described the striking down of the prior; the manner in which his own life had been spared by Count Sidroc; the accident at the ford; and his escape.

Through it all the Prince sat with bowed head and knitted brow, only glancing up now and then to study the face of the boy who told his story so simply and sadly, taking no credit to himself for anything.

"But Heribert found me," cried Turgar, "after he had cut adrift the ships belonging to the Danes. He must tell of that, himself!"

Then the Prince's eyes sought Heribert's face, and the boy, with flushed cheeks, but unflinching truth, told how he had run away from the abbey while Turgar had stayed, of his shame at having done so, and of all his later experiences up to the time of his finding Turgar. "Then together," he added, "we ran to the home of Oswyn and told him of the predicament the Danes were in at the ford, and Oswyn gathered a company of men and has even now gone to the ford to meet the Danes. Then Turgar suggested that we come here and tell the monks. And now they have gone to join Oswyn's forces."

When the story was finished Alfred stood up and looked at the two boys who were on their feet before him. "You are brave lads," he said. As he spoke he caught up his horse's bridle.

Then, for an instant, he stopped. "Before I go," he added, "I want to prove to you that I value your bravery and your help'"

With that the prince took from his own mantle a clasp which he fastened to the shoulder of Heribert's tunic, and from his arm he slipped a bracelet of gold and clasped it upon the arm of Turgar.

The next moment he sprang to his saddle, then turning, he said, "If you catch sight of my men anywhere about, direct them to the ford, and tell them to ride with all speed."

The boys had at first been too overwhelmed with happiness for speech, and indeed the Prince had given them no time for it. But now, as he was about to dash away, there came a sound of shouting and the tramping of many feet.

"The Danes are overthrown! They have paid the price of their bloodthirsty deeds!"

It was the shout of the monks, as they returned to the hermitage of Gyrth.

CHAPTER XII

RESTORING THE TREASURE

Turgar and Heribert had been made happy beyond measure by the gifts of Prince Albert, and two more justly proud and delighted boys could not have been found in all the land of the Saxons.

The rout of the Danes at the ford had been complete. Oswyn's men had surprised them while their arms were laid aside, for they had worked long in trying to repair the broken wagon, and, finding it an impossible task, they had sent away for another wagon into which they were transferring the treasure when they were attacked.

They had, in a measure, recovered from their surprise, and had armed themselves, when the monks arrived with such shouting that it seemed as though this handful of men had been a whole army, for the Danes could hear but could not see them. Before they emerged from the woods, the Danes, thinking that the Saxons were being fully reinforced, left their coveted treasure and ran toward the river, thinking to sail away in their ships and thus at least save their own lives.

But arriving at the point where their ships had been anchored, and finding that all were gone, the men lost all semblance of order and were destroyed by the pursuing Saxons, to a man.

There was great rejoicing in the neighborhood of Gyrth's little home when the monks returned and told their story, and no one rejoiced more heartily than the two boys who had witnessed the terrible cruelty of the Danish horde, and who had been the means of bringing about their punishment.

In spite of their rejoicing over this victory, however, it was a sad company of monks that made its way on the following morning from the hermitage back to the ruined abbey of Crowland. Turgar and Heribert accompanied them.

But they set about their task of burying, of clearing away, and of rebuilding with the determination of men who found a grim satisfaction in building up what the hated Danes had destroyed, and to whom the hardest tasks were far better than idleness.

The boys found much that they could do to help, but how different were the days spent in clearing rubbish or mixing mortar for the masonry, from the former days when they had sung in the chapel choir, studied with the good Prior Theodore, or illumined the letters of a manuscript beside their beloved Friar Joly.

Turgar thought deeply of all these things as he toiled, for after the happenings of the last few days he would never again be the same carefree boy that he had been before. But in spite of the character of the hard work that he was now doing, he realized that a life of physical activity and even of danger, suited him better than the life of a student. He was happier when helping even to build walls and to fashion casements than when reciting Latin chants and translating books, so long as there were Danes in the land, and the people were subject to such attacks as he had witnessed.

"I am glad that I have learned to read and to write," he said one day to Heribert, "but I could not be satisfied to stay here forever. When the abbey is rebuilt, I hope that I may go home."

"If you go, I shall wish to go home, too," answered Heribert.

Their days of peril and excitement had made the two boys fast friends, for each had recognized the true heroism of the other, and their admiration soon turned to a deep and lasting love.

After a moment Turgar asked, "Have you ever heard,

Heribert, what became of the Danish ships after you cut them adrift?"

"Friar Joly told me only this morning," replied Heribert, "that some of Oswyn's men were sent to follow them down the river, and that they captured all of them. One had reached the sea, one had run its prow into a bank and was held fast, while the others were at the mouth of the river. They were all delivered over to the King."

"You will be rewarded for that some day," said Turgar.

"This is reward enough," replied Heribert simply, touching the clasp on the shoulder of his tunic.

Turgar laid his hand with a gesture of affection upon his bracelet. "I like to feel it there," he said, "and to know that it has been upon the arm of Prince Alfred. It gives me greater courage for every sort of duty. Though I hope," he continued, with a laugh, "that the duty may not always be that of mixing mortar."

Heribert laughed, too, as he started away with a bucket of the despised mortar upon his shoulder.

Slowly the abbey began to take on something of its former appearance, and at last the walls were completed, the altar replaced, and the work of restoration finished.

Then a day was set apart for certain of the monks

to go to the hermitage of Gyrth and bring back the hidden treasure. Friar Joly headed the little band, and at his request Turgar and Heribert were permitted to go with them.

To the monks this return of the treasure was a solemn festival, but to the two boys it seemed more like an adventure, for they were glad of the change of occupation and of scene. Then, too, there was always the need of looking out for Danes, although none had been reported in that part of the country for some time.

Their trip to the hermitage was without special adventure, and the company was warmly greeted by Gyrth. After a simple ceremony, they began the actual work of unearthing the hidden treasure.

Friar Joly saw that the boys were equipped with tools for the work, and instructed them to use the greatest care so that no injury should be done the precious vessels.

"Here is the spot," said Turgar, as he and Heribert reached a certain tree. "Under this gnarled branch, the friar told me that we would find certain of the pieces." He knelt as he spoke and pushed aside the leaves and leaf mold, revealing beneath it the unmistakable signs of freshly turned earth.

Then the boys began digging, but the treasure was not deeply covered.

"Carefully now!" cried Heribert. Then, together, they worked with their hands to remove the remaining earth.

"Ah," exclaimed Turgar a moment later, holding up a heavy golden goblet, "this seems always to fall to my lot, and I am glad!" Then, as they worked, he told Heribert the story of King Arthur and his Knights, as Friar Joly had told it to him, though he knew the story more fully now, for he had read about it, and had asked many questions since he had first heard the tale.

"And this," he added, as he completed his story "once belonged to King Arthur. I wonder if Sir Lancelot or Sir Galahad ever drank from it."

"I would like to have lived in those days, and to have followed King Arthur," said Heribert. "I wonder if there were Danes to fight in those days, too."

"There were Saxons to fight in those days," replied Turgar, with a laugh, "and, from what I am told, they must have been nearly as bad as the Danes."

"How so?" exclaimed Heribert warmly, for Heribert had spent less time in study than Turgar,

"The early Saxons, you know, were heathen, and they worshiped the gods of Asgard, just as the Danes do now. They, too, came from the Northland, and were fierce pirates as well as terrible fighters."

"Then King Arthur and his Knights were not Saxons?" asked Heribert.

"No, they were Britons, and the Saxons conquered them and settled upon their land."

"Well, if that is the case," responded Heribert, "I think I am quite as well satisfied to fight with Prince Alfred against the Danes. I have no love for the Britons. But I don't like your comparing the Saxons with the Danes!"

"It isn't a nice comparison, I admit," agreed Turgar, "but look it up for yourself. The books in the abbey tell about it. They say that it is the Christian religion that has changed the nature of the Saxons, and that it would do the same for the Danes if they would accept it."

"That is hard to believe of the Danes," replied Heribert, as he replaced the last shovelful of earth, and Turgar, gathering up his share of the treasure, responded, "That is true; but it probably is just what the Britons said about the Saxons long years ago."

CHAPTER XIII
"My King"

The monastery at Crowland had been rebuilt, so far as it had been possible for the monks to restore it, and its treasures had been returned.

Once more the candles burned upon its altars, and psalms and anthems were chanted. The usual routine of monastery life was again established, though with sadly diminished ranks.

The boys resumed the study of lessons and tried faithfully to keep their minds upon translations and texts, but it was difficult for both.

"I tell you, Turgar," Heribert said one day, "I am no student, and there is no use in trying to make me one. I would far rather handle a spear than a paint brush, and even during prayers my mind is off with the soldiers."

"It is hard to settle down to life in the abbey after having that experience with the Danes," responded Turgar. "I have always said I was too active to lead the life of a monk. If I were older I would not remain here another day. But what can two boys do?"

"Well, sometimes they can do quite a bit, when they get a chance," replied Heribert significantly.

"Yes, that is true," assented Turgar. "But for myself, I have concluded to stay and learn all that I can in the abbey until I am old enough to serve the Prince. I hope our country may not always have the Danes to fight, and in times of peace the knowledge we gain here will be good to have."

"I suppose you are right," answered Heribert, "and I shall try not to waste my time while I must stay."

But neither boy dreamed how soon his quiet life at the abbey was to come to an end.

A few days later there was great commotion in the abbey, caused by the arrival of a solitary soldier. He proved to be a young chief of the Saxon army, bearing news of a recent battle. He was dressed in shining armor of gilded scales from which the rays of the western sun were reflected in countless flashes of light. His sheathed sword hung by his side. On his arms were many bracelets of gold, and a golden torque was about his neck. So splendid a figure the boys had never seen. Even Prince Alfred was not so splendidly equipped when he rode to the hermitage of Gyrth.

The monks gathered quickly about the newly arrived

warrior, for they felt sure that he must be the bearer of important news.

He did not wait to be questioned. Raising his shining helmet, he said, "I have come from battle. Ethelred, the King, is sorely wounded."

The faces of the monks grew pale; then their cheeks flushed, and their eyes flashed. "Where are the Danes?" demanded Friar Joly.

"They have fled to their fortified stronghold by the river. But the victory is with the Saxons, and only a remnant of the Danes escaped."

"Praise God for that!" exclaimed the monks earnestly and reverently.

Then, briefly, the young chief told of the events of the battle: how Ethelred had held solemn services in his tent before he led his division of the army into battle: how the young Prince Alfred had stood in the thickest of the fight, encouraging and strengthening the men of his division: of how, together, the Saxons had overcome the heathen horde and driven them back with great slaughter. It was a mighty victory for the Saxons—but Ethelred, their King, was badly wounded.

After the soldier had ridden away to bear his message to other places, his news remained the one topic of conversation at the abbey, and there was great rejoicing at the overthrow of the Danes.

A few days later, as Turgar was engaged Upon his lessons with Friar Joly, he suddenly asked, "Do you think the Danes will dare make another attack? Are they not fully conquered now?"

Friar Joly shook his head. "The Danes are like swarms of troublesome insects," he said. "When one swarm is crushed, another comes from the north to take its place."

Turgar had seldom seen the jovial friar so downcast, and he resumed his translation with a feeling of impending trouble.

He was struggling with a Latin phrase, when the friar said, "Turgar, listen. Something impels me to tell you what is in my heart. I have thought much about these matters, and prayed much. I believe that some day Alfred will be made King of the Saxons. He is young now, but, young as he is, he is the greatest man amongst us. He is a thinker. He is not ruled by passion. If he becomes ruler in fact, he will have a terrible task before him, but I believe that in the end he will conquer the Danes, and bring peace to this sorely afflicted land. It will be a great victory, and he will be a great King.

"I do not know why I tell you this," Friar Joly added, as he looked down into Turgar's shining eyes.

"Perhaps," answered Turgar softly, "it is because I love the Prince so well."

A few weeks later another messenger arrived at the monastery. He, too, was a soldier, but not dressed in such wonderful armor. But as he rode into the court, Turgar, who was crossing it, looked up, and then gave a great cry of joy. "Withgar!"

Truly it was Withgar, his brother, come to Crowland to bring news of great importance. Turgar ran to him, and Withgar sprang from his horse and folded the boy in a strong embrace. He told him news of home, of Wulstan, of Gyneth, and even of Wulf his dog. Then, as the monks crowded about, he addressed the whole company.

"I have sad news to unfold," he said, "for Ethelred, the King, is dead." There was a hush over all the band, as Withgar gave some details of the King's illness, resulting from the wound he had received in the battle with the Danes.

"A successor has been chosen," Withgar continued, and all waited in breathless silence as he added, "Prince Alfred will succeed him."

"And not his eldest son!" exclaimed the prior.

"No," said Withgar, "the times are too filled with peril for a young and untried ruler to be placed in power. Alfred has for many years been ruler in all but name.

They Found It Hard To Bid Good-Bye To The Monks.

Now he is to be ruler in fact. It was the wish of his father, King Ethelwolf, that Albert, his youngest son, should succeed Ethelred, his oldest son, and when he was little more than a babe the Pope declared Albert would yet be King."

Turgar's eyes sought those of Friar Joly, as he whispered to himself, "My Prince! And now he is a King!"

When the voices, raised in comment and in exclamation, had somewhat subsided, Withgar spoke again. "I have yet another message to deliver," he said, "and one that I count it a joy to be able to bring in person. I come directly from the court of King Alfred, and I am commissioned to return there with two youths whose names are Turgar and Heribert.

The two boys could scarcely believe their ears. What could it mean?

"The new King had need of pages," continued Withgar, while his eyes rested upon Turgar's flushed face, "and, first of all, he has named these two."

A murmur of approval went up from the company of monks. Turgar felt such a surging joy that at first he could not speak. At last he exclaimed, "But how did he happen to choose us?"

"Such things do not happen, Turgar," said Friar Joly,

whose face was wreathed in smiles over the happiness of his favorite pupil.

"King Alfred told me a story," said Withgar, "of the work you two boys did the night the monastery was burned. He called it 'man's work,' and he said that you were the sort of boys he wanted to have about him, and to have trained for his service."

"Heribert! can you believe it?" cried Turgar, grasping his friend's arm.

"It seems altogether too good to be true," answered Heribert with shining eyes.

But when, at Withgar's bidding, they went to prepare themselves for the journey to the court, they found it hard to bid good-bye to the monks who had been their friends for so many months, and with whom they shared so many sad and tender memories. It was especially hard to take leave of Friar Joly, but, as they rode away, his was the last face that they saw, and his the last voice that they heard, calling, "God be with you, my boys. I know you will be faithful pages to Alfred the King."

THE END.

www.ingramcontent.com/pod-product-compliance
Lightning Source LLC
Chambersburg PA
CBHW021339060726
47591CB00006B/2088